little Miss Trouble

by Roger Hargreaves

"Here comes trouble," people used to say.

And who do you think would come walking along?

That's right!

Little Miss Trouble.

Oh, the trouble she caused.

One morning she went to see Mr Uppity.

"Do you know what Mr Small calls you behind your back?" she asked him.

"No," replied Mr Uppity.

"What does Mr Small call me behind my back?"

Little Miss Trouble looked at him.

"Fatty!" she said.

Now, Mr Uppity didn't like that.

Not at all.

Not one little bit.

He went round immediately to see Mr Small.

"How dare you call me FATTY?" he shouted.

"But…" stammered Mr Small, who never had called him 'Fatty'.

"But…"

"But nothing," shouted Mr Uppity.

And he hit poor Mr Small.

Ouch!

And gave him a black eye.

Poor Mr Small.

Little Miss Trouble, who was hiding behind a tree, hugged herself with glee.

"Oh, I do so like making trouble," she giggled to herself.

Naughty girl!

Little Miss Trouble went to see Mr Clever.

"Do you know what Mr Small calls you behind your back?" she asked him.

"No," replied Mr Clever.

"Tell me! What does Mr Small call me behind my back?"

Little Miss Trouble looked at him.

"Big Nose!" she said.

Now.

Mr Clever didn't like that very much either.

Off he rushed.

And, when he found Mr Small, without waiting for an explanation, he punched him!

Hard!

In the other eye!

Poor Mr Small.

Two black eyes for something he'd never done.

"Oh look at you," Miss Trouble laughed when she saw him.

"It's all your fault," said Mr Small.

"True," she said.

And walked off.

Poor Mr Small had to go to the doctor.

"Good heavens!" exclaimed Doctor Makeyouwell when he saw him. "Whatever happened to you?"

Mr Small explained.

"I think," Doctor Makeyouwell said when he'd heard what Mr Small had to tell him, "that something should be done about that little lady! What she needs is..."

Then he stopped.

And he chuckled.

"That's it," he laughed.

"What's it?" asked Mr Small.

And Doctor Makeyouwell whispered something to Mr Small.

Would you like to know what he whispered?

Not telling you!

It's a secret!

That afternoon Mr Small went to see Mr Tickle.

"Do you know what Miss Trouble calls you behind your back?" he asked.

"No," said Mr Tickle.

"What does Miss Trouble call me behind my back?"

Mr Small looked at him.

"Pudding Face!" he said.

Then Mr Small went to see Mr Bump.

"Do you know what Miss Trouble calls you behind your back?" he asked.

"No," said Mr Bump.

"What does Miss Trouble call me behind my back?"

Mr Small looked at him.

"Mr Nitwit!" he said.

Little Miss Trouble was in trouble.

"How dare you call me 'Pudding Face'?"
cried Mr Tickle.

And tickled her.

"And how dare you call me 'Mr Nitwit'?"
cried Mr Bump.

And bumped her.

Now, I don't know whether you've ever been
tickled and bumped at the same time, but it's
not much fun.

In fact it's no fun at all.

Ticklebumpticklebumpticklebumpticklebump!

For ten minutes.

And ten minutes of ticklebumping is a long
time.

I can tell you!

Later that evening Doctor Makeyouwell strolled round to see Mr Small.

"How are the eyes?" he asked.

"Oh much better now thank you," replied Mr Small.

"And did our little plan work?" asked the doctor.

"It did indeed," grinned Mr Small.

"Shake," said Doctor Makeyouwell.

And they shook hands.

Well.

Not quite hands.

Doctor Makeyouwell then strolled round to see Miss Trouble.

She was feeling very sorry for herself.

"What's wrong with you?" he asked her.

And she told him all about it.

All about everything.

Doctor Makeyouwell looked at her.

"Cheer up," he said.

"You know what you've just had, don't you?"

Little Miss Trouble shook her head.

"A taste of your own medicine," he chuckled.

And went home.

For supper.

3 Great Offers for MR. MEN Fans!

MR. MEN TOKEN

1 New Mr. Men or Little Miss Library Bus Presentation Cases

A brand new stronger, roomier school bus library box, with sturdy carrying handle and stay-closed fasteners.

The full colour, wipe-clean boxes make a great home for your full collection.

They're just £5.99 inc P&P and free bookmark!

☐ MR. MEN   ☐ LITTLE MISS (please tick and order overleaf)

2 Door Hangers and Posters

In every Mr. Men and Little Miss book like this one, you will find a special token. Collect 6 tokens and we will send you a brilliant Mr. Men or Little Miss poster and a Mr. Men or Little Miss double sided full colour bedroom door hanger of your choice. Simply tick your choice in the list and tape a 50p coin for your two items to this page.

PLEASE STICK YOUR 50P COIN HERE

Door Hangers (please tick)
☐ Mr. Nosey & Mr. Muddle
☐ Mr. Slow & Mr. Busy
☐ Mr. Messy & Mr. Quiet
☐ Mr. Perfect & Mr. Forgetful
☐ Little Miss Fun & Little Miss Late
☐ Little Miss Helpful & Little Miss Tidy
☐ Little Miss Busy & Little Miss Brainy
☐ Little Miss Star & Little Miss Fun

Posters (please tick)
☐ MR.MEN
☐ LITTLE MISS

3 Sixteen Beautiful Fridge Magnets – any 2 for £2.00! inc. P&P

They're very special collector's items!
Simply tick your first and second* choices from the list below of any 2 characters!

1st Choice
- [ ] Mr. Happy
- [ ] Mr. Lazy
- [ ] Mr. Topsy-Turvy
- [ ] Mr. Bounce
- [ ] Mr. Bump
- [ ] Mr. Small
- [ ] Mr. Snow
- [ ] Mr. Wrong
- [ ] Mr. Daydream
- [ ] Mr. Tickle
- [ ] Mr. Greedy
- [ ] Mr. Funny
- [ ] Little Miss Giggles
- [ ] Little Miss Splendid
- [ ] Little Miss Naughty
- [ ] Little Miss Sunshine

2nd Choice
- [ ] Mr. Happy
- [ ] Mr. Lazy
- [ ] Mr. Topsy-Turvy
- [ ] Mr. Bounce
- [ ] Mr. Bump
- [ ] Mr. Small
- [ ] Mr. Snow
- [ ] Mr. Wrong
- [ ] Mr. Daydream
- [ ] Mr. Tickle
- [ ] Mr. Greedy
- [ ] Mr. Funny
- [ ] Little Miss Giggles
- [ ] Little Miss Splendid
- [ ] Little Miss Naughty
- [ ] Little Miss Sunshine

*Only in case your first choice is out of stock.

--- TO BE COMPLETED BY AN ADULT ---

To apply for any of these great offers, ask an adult to complete the coupon below and send it with the appropriate payment and tokens, if needed, to MR. MEN CLASSIC OFFER, PO BOX 715, HORSHAM RH12 5WG

- [ ] Please send ____ Mr. Men Library case(s) and/or ____ Little Miss Library case(s) at £5.99 each inc P&P
- [ ] Please send a poster and door hanger, as selected overleaf. I enclose six tokens plus a 50p coin for P&P
- [ ] Please send me ____ pair(s) of Mr. Men/Little Miss fridge magnets, as selected above at £2.00 inc P&P

Fan's Name _____

Address _____

_____ **Postcode** _____

Date of Birth _____

Name of Parent/Guardian _____

Total amount enclosed £ _____

- [ ] I enclose a cheque/postal order payable to Egmont Books Limited
- [ ] **Please charge my MasterCard/Visa/Amex/Switch or Delta account** (delete as appropriate)

Card Number

Expiry date ___/___   **Signature** _____

Please allow 28 days for delivery. Offer is only available while stocks last. We reserve the right to change the terms of this offer at any time and we offer a 14 day money back guarantee. This does not affect your statutory rights.
Data Protection Act: If you do not wish to receive other similar offers from us or companies we recommend, please tick this box [ ]. Offers apply to UK only.

MR.MEN   LITTLE MISS
Mr. Men and Little Miss™ & ©Mrs. Roger Hargreaves